W9-AFR-703

# LOST IN BERMOODA

written and illustrated by

MIKE LITWIN

ALBERT WHITMAN & COMPANY
CHICAGO, ILLINOIS

for Xander

Library of Congress Cataloging-in-Publication data is on file with the publisher.

Published in 2014 by Albert Whitman & Company
ISBN 978-0-8075-8718-8

Printed in China.
10 9 8 7 6 5 4 3 2 1 BP 18 17 16 15 14 13

For more information about Albert Whitman & Company, visit our web site at www.albertwhitman.com.

# CONTENTS

It was another perfect afternoon on the island of Bermooda. The sun was perfectly bright, the breeze was perfectly warm, and the waves sounded perfectly lovely as they rolled upon the soft, sandy beach. It was all perfect, just like every other day. It was the kind of perfection that made it seem like nothing in this tropical paradise could ever change. But life *was* about to change, and it would all start with a shout.

"Chuck! Come back! You're not supposed to go down there!"

Patty Porter chased after her brother, who was quickly making his way down the cliff to the Boneyard. That was the one place on the whole island where their mother had told the two calves *not* to go. "Come back here or I'm telling Mama! Do you hear me?" Patty yelled.

Chuck heard her just fine, but he didn't stop. "Come on, don't be such a scaredy-cow!" he yelled back. "Besides, it's the middle of the day. What could happen? I'm going, with or without you."

"Fine! You can go *without* me!" Patty huffed. Off she trotted, until she and her pink flowered dress disappeared into the palm trees. Chuck didn't care. Patty was always getting him in trouble anyway. Today he had bigger things on his mind. Today he was going to find a trinket.

Now Chuck would never admit this, but the Boneyard was a spooky place, even in the daytime. Chuck could almost feel ghostly things watching him as he tiptoed around the ancient shipwreck resting quietly in the sand. The cows of Bermooda called this shipwreck "the Boneyard" because its massive timbers jutted out of the ground like some giant, creepy skeleton.

Most of the wreck had been moved up to the island's museum, but sometimes—if you were lucky—you could still find a little something buried in the sand. Something interesting. Something mysterious. Something left over from those legendary creatures called "hu'mans." *A trinket.* That's what he was looking for today.

The little cow poked a boat paddle around in the sand searching for stuff that he thought might be from the old shipwreck. After an hour or so, he stretched out his blanket and carefully placed all of the items he found on top. He wrinkled his nose and frowned as he surveyed his collection. All he had was a chunk of driftwood, a broken clamshell, three blunt whale teeth, and a sea sponge that looked a lot like a snout.

"Rats!" he mumbled. Last month, his whole class had been so impressed when Muster Cloverhoof brought in the old hu'man spoon he found in the Boneyard. After all, it was a

daring thing for a calf to venture down into this haunted place. How could Chuck go back with nothing to show for it?

He had hoped to find something that would impress everyone and win a few friends. Chuck didn't have many friends. He liked to think it was because he was such a daring loner, but it was really because he spent much of his time daydreaming and talking about places that didn't exist. He imagined fantastic worlds over the horizon, far beyond the quiet shores of Bermooda.

This old shipwreck made him think of the amazing world the hu'mans must have come from. He had hoped that coming to the Boneyard would lead to something exciting, but so far he had found nothing but junk on an empty beach.

"There's no adventure here," he grumbled to himself. "Not in the Boneyard or anywhere else on this boring island."

Then he saw something odd. Way out across the shallow pool inside the shoals, the waves were breaking funny. Something—or someone—was lying on one of the sandbars! Chuck hadn't found anything on the beach and he did not want to go home empty-hooved. Should he dare go out there and see what it was? A warm breeze tickled his snout. He twitched his tail as he wondered.

Chuck pulled a plank from the shipwreck and dragged it to the shore. He bunched up his blanket full of junk and put it on the plank. He sat on the plank behind the blanket bundle and paddled the board like a canoe across the calm water. As he floated closer to the sandbar, he started to worry about what he would find there. Was it just a piece of a boat? An injured cow? A hungry shark playing dead? By the time Chuck reached the sand, he was terrified.

Chuck slowly inched closer to the lumpy blob lying in the surf. It wasn't very big. In fact, it was about the same size as him. He raised his paddle slowly and carefully. His paddle hovered inches above the lump and was just close enough to tap the blob ever so gently. He gave the lump a firm nudge, and—

Nothing! It didn't move at all. Whatever it

was, it looked dead as it just laid there on top of a floating orange ring. Chuck leaned in close to get a better look. Somehow, this thing felt familiar. It was some kind of animal, but it was definitely not a shark. It was wearing a shirt like him, but it was definitely not a cow. It had no horns, no hooves, and no sharp teeth. This thing was soft and pink and about the same size as him. Arms, legs, some yellow hair…

Chuck gasped when he suddenly realized what this thing was. In his shock, he lost his balance and stumbled, falling face down in the water and waking up the creature in front of him. He lifted his snout from the sea foam and found himself staring face-to-face with the most terrifying thing he'd ever seen.

The creature let out a loud scream. Chuck let out a shrieking moo. The creature dove under the orange ring. Chuck rushed out of the water. He grabbed his blanket and scrambled under it, scattering his junk collection all over the ground.

He had gone in search of a hu'man trinket. But instead he found a real, live hu'man!

"Don't eat me!" Chuck cried. Cowering beneath his blanket, he wept and wailed and wished he'd never gone to the Boneyard. He had never seen a creature like this in all his life.

He'd read about them in his history books. He'd seen their tools in the museum. He'd drawn them from his imagination. But no one he knew had ever seen one in real life before.

This was a cow-eating, bone-crunching, fire-breathing hu'man! A *real* one!

But after a few minutes, Chuck couldn't help but notice that he had, in fact, not been eaten yet. He peeked out from under his blanket to see the hu'man still hiding under its ring.

*Why is that thing hiding?* Chuck asked himself. *Why hasn't it eaten me?* Then another thought occurred to him. *Why am I hiding? This isn't what a brave adventurer would do!*

Chuck gathered all his courage and cast off his blanket. Grabbing his boat paddle, he ran toward the monster with his face scrunched up tight to look like he wasn't afraid.

"Don't eat me!" the hu'man cried out.

Chuck paused. What? Wasn't that what he

just said? Was this thing...*afraid* of him?

"Who are you?" Chuck demanded. "What are you doing here?"

"Where am I?" the thing looked around.

"Never mind!" Chuck snapped. "I know what you are! You're a hu'man! A monster! You're here to scorch me with fire and eat me for dinner! Well, not if I have anything to do with it!" Chuck felt bolder and bolder as this monster trembled in the sand.

He shook his paddle in the thing's face to let him know who was boss. "What is your name, *hu'man*?" he bellowed. But the hu'man just stared at him with wide eyes, breathing shakily. And then something really strange happened—the monster began to cry.

"Hey," Chuck said, lowering his paddle. "Hey, don't cry. Stop it! Monsters don't cry."

"I'm not a monster," the thing blubbered. "I'm just a kid! Please don't eat me!"

Chuck looked down at the weeping hu'man and felt very confused. For nine years, all he had ever heard was that hu'mans were terrible cow-eating monsters. But this thing didn't look like any monster Chuck had imagined. It didn't breathe fire. It didn't have a pointy tail or long fangs. This thing was lost and confused and scared that Chuck was going to eat him!

"Hey," Chuck said again. "It's all right. Look, I'm not going to hurt you. See? Come on, look at me."

The hu'man looked up at him with a tear-streaked face. "You're...a talking cow!"

Chuck curled his nose and raised an eyebrow. What a silly thing to say. "Of course I can talk. Can't everyone?" He sat down in the sand next to the terrified hu'man.

"I'm Chuck Porter," he said, holding out a hoof. "Welcome to Bermooda."

The hu'man slowly reached his hand out

and shook Chuck's hoof. He looked around him like he was searching for something and then finally said, "Umm…Dakota. My name is Dakota. Where did you say I am?"

"Bermooda," Chuck repeated. "It's an island. I live with my family right over there," he said, pointing a hoof over his shoulder.

The hu'man looked down the coastline. It was thick with green trees and colorful flowers. Jewel-green waves rushed along its gleaming white beaches. Behind the trees, a giant mountain stretched up into the bright blue sky. Everything was lush and beautiful. It looked like…paradise.

"Is everyone here a cow like you?" he asked.

"Not everyone," Chuck said. "There are

pigs, monkeys, birds…all kinds of folks. But I can say there's no one on this island like you. Where did you come from?"

There was a long pause before Dakota answered. "Umm. I was on a boat with my family. Yeah, we were out in the ocean, and I guess I just…fell off."

Chuck looked at Dakota's soft pink fingers and toes. He still did not understand why this hu'man did not look as fearsome as he expected.

"Where are your claws?" Chuck asked.

"I don't have any claws," Dakota answered.

"What about fire? Can you breathe fire?"

"I don't think so."

Chuck let out a disappointed sigh. So far,

hu'mans were not turning out to be very impressive. "Well, what can you do?"

Dakota thought for a moment, then stuck out his tongue and touched it to the tip of his nose. "I can do that."

Chuck grinned and touched his tongue to his own nose. "Me too!"

The two of them laughed. What an odd thing to have in common!

"So...are there more hu'mans out there?" Chuck asked excitedly.

"Sure," Dakota said. "Lots of them."

"Tell me more!" Chuck begged.

They sat in the sand while Dakota told Chuck more about the hu'man world. It was an unbelievable place filled with moving pictures on glowing screens and buildings so tall they scraped the sky. It was the kind of world Chuck had only dreamed of.

"Do they have any cows there?" Chuck asked.

"Umm...well," Dakota thought it'd be best not to mention what life is like for cows back home. So after a short pause he said, "No. Not really."

Chuck was finding himself wonderfully entertained, and he decided at once that this hu'man must come home with him. He thought it would be rather amazing to have his very own hu'man. Even if it was just for a little while.

"Okay, Dakota," Chuck said, getting

back up on his hooves. "You're coming home with me." He began collecting his junk back up in the blanket.

"Home? With you?" Dakota asked, with a look of disbelief.

"Well, you can't stay here." Chuck said as he dragged the plank back to the edge of the sandbar. "But you can stay with my family until we find a way to get you back to your home."

Dakota really wasn't sure what to do, but he knew this talking cow was right. It was getting late and he couldn't stay here on this sandbar forever. So he climbed onto the wooden plank with Chuck and paddled back to the beach.

They were about to climb the hill leaving the Boneyard when Chuck had a sudden thought.

"Wait!" he said. "We'll have to hide you. They'll never understand."

"They who?" Dakota asked.

"The herd," Chuck said. "They're the cows who lead Bermooda. A council. They make all the laws and big decisions. I don't know what they'll do if they find out there's a hu'man on the island!" Chuck's tail twitched as he thought for a moment. "I've got an idea! We'll make you some cowmaflague."

"Cow-ma-what?" Dakota repeated.

"A disguise!" Chuck said. He dumped the driftwood, clamshell, whale's teeth, and sea sponge back onto the ground and began tearing his fuzzy blanket. "We're going to turn you into a cow!"

"There's no way this is going to work."

Dakota clomped along in the disguise Chuck had made. Strips of Chuck's blanket had been torn and pieced together into what looked like cow pajamas, complete with a hood and a swishy little tail. Coconut shells had been cut to look like hooves and tied to the outsides of his hands and feet. Chuck used the whale teeth he had found to make horn

buds, and the sea sponge was tied like a mask across Dakota's face.

It was terrible. When Dakota looked down, he didn't see a cow. He saw a kid wearing a horribly stitched cow costume.

"Leave everything to me," Chuck said. "I have a plan. Just relax. Don't walk so fast. And try not to sweat so much. Cows don't sweat like that."

Dakota wasn't sure how to relax with Chuck giving him so many orders. And how could he make himself sweat less? After a long walk that seemed to last forever, they finally stopped at a bush of hibiscus flowers underneath a wooden sign that read, *The Porter House*.

Behind the sign stood the craziest-looking house Dakota had ever seen. There were lots of windows, boardwalks, and odd-shaped rooms sticking out all over the place. It looked like a bunch of shacks and bamboo huts had all been stuck together to make one big mega-house. It was huge.

"Wow!" Dakota said. "You must have a really big family."

"Porters aren't the only ones living here,"

Chuck explained. "It's our house, but there's lots of extra rooms and other folks have lived in them for years."

Chuck and Dakota had arrived just in time for dinner. They entered to find that everyone had already taken their seats at the long dinner table. In addition to cows, lots of other animals had gathered for the meal, including a small green parrot with a nervous twitch, an old gray porcupine with glasses, and a manic orange monkey who couldn't seem to stop laughing.

"Everyone, this is Dakota." Chuck said. "He's…visiting."

"Visiting? From where?" Chuck's sister Patty asked. "Why haven't I seen you at school?"

"His family doesn't live on the island." Chuck said. "They live on a boat. Out at sea. He's a…sea cow. Can he stay with us for a little while, Mama?"

Mama Porter's eyes were kind and loving. She had a warm smile that almost made Dakota feel right at home, even as he stood there trying not to sweat. She didn't seem suspicious of him at all. Was she really fooled by this costume?

"Well, Dakota, it's a pleasure to have you,"

she said in a gentle voice. "We're about to have dinner if you'll join us."

Chuck and Dakota sat down at the table, which had a delicious-looking spread of dates, nuts, apples, bananas, mangoes, corn, and tomatoes. Dakota's stomach growled. With everything that had happened today, Dakota had forgotten how hungry he was.

Across the table from Dakota sat an older lady cow in a very tidy dress, with her napkin perfectly folded in her lap. She offered a bowl of dates to the small green parrot perched next to her. "Would you like some dates, Ditto?"

Ditto was an awfully loud and squawky bird, and he never seemed to start a sentence without repeating the last thing someone

else said. "Would I like some dates? Would I? Would I? Yes! Thank you, Miss Magnolia! Moohalo!" He dove his beak into the bowl as Miss Magnolia smiled.

Chuck passed a bowl of bright green grass blades to Dakota.

"What's this?" Dakota whispered.

"Bermooda grass," Chuck said.

"I can't eat this!" he whispered back, a little too loudly. Everyone at the table stopped eating and looked at Dakota.

"What I mean is…I'm…umm…allergic. Allergic to Bermooda grass," Dakota sputtered out. "Could I just have some fruit, please?"

"You must have a very unique family, Dakota," said the elderly porcupine as Dakota munched on an apple. He peered at Dakota through his glasses. "Living on the water... allergic to Bermooda grass...and I don't think I've ever seen a cow with blue eyes before. And you seem to be more fuzzy than furry."

Dakota cleared his throat and laughed nervously. This spiny porcupine was just as sharp as he looked. "Yes, sir, we're umm... kind of a different breed."

*Yeah,* Chuck thought to himself. *A really different breed.*

"Now, Quincy," Miss Magnolia scolded the old porcupine, "that's no proper way to treat a guest. Guests should be treated with as much respect as the Wellingtons themselves."

"Who are the Wellingtons?" Dakota asked.

"Who are the Wellingtons?" Ditto repeated loudly. "You don't know who the Wellingtons are?"

"Dakota's a sea cow," Chuck said. "The Wellingtons don't own the sea."

"Why not? They own everything else," snorted Chuck's Uncle Bo, a sloppy-looking cow with a huge belly that shook when he talked. "They own the grass fields, the coconut grove, the windspinners...plenty of moo'lah in that family."

"We're quite blessed with what we have," Mama Porter cut in. "We have our family, our friends, and our pride. That's good enough for me."

"Me too! That's good enough for me!" Ditto echoed.

"Indeed," Quincy agreed.

"Sounds like a right proper attitude," said Miss Magnolia, nodding her head.

"Did anyone hear that Wilhelm Wellington today?" Uncle Bo continued. Bermooda grass fell out of his mouth as he spoke. "He was at the herd meeting this afternoon, talking about *hu'mans*. Trying to get everyone into a stampede. He even said there might be one here on the island. Can you believe that?"

Everyone around the table chuckled, except for Chuck and Dakota. Dakota was now sweating more than ever.

"What if he's right?" Chuck asked. "What if there really is a hu'man here? What would the herd do?"

Uncle Bo's chuckle erupted into an all-out guffaw. "You've gotta be kidding! What an idea! There's no such thing as hu'mans!" He threw himself back in his chair, holding his belly and laughing so hard he almost choked on his Bermooda grass. "*Hu'mans!* What a joke!"

The orange monkey cackled wildly along with Uncle Bo. "Hahahahaha! Hu'mans!" he screeched. "You're a great jokester, Chuck!"

Chuck looked defeated and Dakota wasn't sure he understood the joke.

***

After dinner, Chuck took Dakota upstairs to his room to get ready for bed. Chuck's room was small and cozy. Next to the bed was a bamboo table that held a small wooden box with pearly knobs and a glass globe with a metal key. A hammock hung in one corner of the room, and on the wall was a poster of a big blue cow holding a surfboard.

"Museum trip at school tomorrow," Papa Porter called from downstairs. "No sunglobes or chatterboxes after nine o'clock. No reason to use up all that boltage."

"Boltage?" Dakota looked very confused.

Chuck explained, "Boltage is like the lightning in a storm, but it's made by windspinners. It comes into the house through here." He pointed to a socket on the floor. "We don't use it for much. Just for sunglobes."

Chuck turned the key on the glass globe, which filled the room with a faint warm glow.

"And chatterboxes." He turned a knob on the wooden box, and a voice came out: *Hey, this is Angus Atkins, bringing you all the best island news and music…*

A sense of joy ran through Dakota as he realized what he was looking at. Light bulbs! Radios! Electricity!

"A-ha! Hahaha! Power!" Dakota laughed with delight and relief. Finally, something he recognized!

"Shhhhh!" Chuck looked at Dakota sideways. "Good gravy, man! Do all hu'mans love power as much as you?"

The next morning, Chuck and Dakota walked to the schoolhouse in Bermooda Village. Planted on the north side of the island, Bermooda Village stretched from the edge of Mount Maverick to the calm, gleaming shore of Bullhorn Bay. The bay was bordered by Cape Cattle and Cape Cud—twin beaches that started at opposite sides of town and reached far out into the sea.

The village itself was a bustling center of activity. A whirlwind of cows, pigs, and oxen surrounded Dakota as they trotted to and fro. The village's simple cobblestone streets were lined with all kinds of shops and stands, and some of the roads even climbed up to buildings that were neatly nestled on the side of the mountain.

The grandest building in town was the Hortica Center, a big museum at the base of the mountain. This is where Chuck and Dakota were visiting today. They stood inside the museum with a class of calves, listening to a speech from a tropical screech owl who sat on a bamboo perch underneath a brass sign that read, *HMS Hortica*.

"Many years ago, a ship crashed here on Bermooda," the owl said. "A slave ship that herded your ancestors across the waves to satisfy the appetite of a bloodthirsty race of creatures known as hu'mans."

"Who's the owl?" Dakota whispered to Chuck.

"That's Cornelius," Chuck whispered back. "He runs the museum. He knows pretty much everything there is to know about Bermooda, and all about hu'mans too."

Cornelius could only be described as stuffy. His puffy gray chest stuck out from his body of fluffy brown feathers. Over his left eye, he wore a gold monocle that never seemed to stay in place. He spoke in a very proper voice and rarely looked directly at anyone.

"Thankfully, the hu'mans all disappeared during the crash," Cornelius continued. "The *HMS Hortica*—whose ruins we now stand in—came to rest at the southern tip of the island, in that wretched place called the Boneyard. It was then that your species came aboard the island to live with the rest of us."

Dakota knew that Cornelius was saying something important, but all he could think of was how hot and scratchy his cowmaflauge was. He pulled and tugged on it, until Chuck put a hoof on his arm.

"Don't attract attention to yourself," Chuck warned Dakota. "Just keep quiet and try not to say anything."

"Cows, pigs, and oxen are not all that arrived with the Hortica," Cornelius went on. "Even though no hu'mans ever came upon the island, many of their books and instruments did."

Dakota looked around. Indeed, the inside of this museum looked much like the inside of an old sailing ship: books, tools, globes, clocks, a spyglass. It looked as if nearly anything that could have been salvaged from the shipwreck had been brought here. "From these, we have learned to read, write, speak, sail, farm, and form a society in which we can all flourish."

As Cornelius spoke, Dakota and the calves began paging through the books on display. There were books about science, astronomy, and art...but the one that really seemed to catch everyone's interest was a big book titled *The Art of Cookery*.

Everyone on Bermooda was familiar with *The Art of Cookery*. That was because nearly every creature on the island was in there somewhere. Everyone knew the page numbers on which they appeared, along with detailed instructions on how they could be plucked, sheared, baked, broiled, stewed, fried, or roasted and served with a garnish. It was the kind of thing that made your fur stand up on the back of your neck.

"Cornelius?" asked a dainty girl cow raising her hoof. "How old is Bermooda?"

"Excellent question, Miss Daisy," Cornelius said, "and my most educated answer is…I don't know." The calves all snickered. It wasn't often that Cornelius didn't know something.

"No one really knows how long the island has been here," he admitted. "Long before your species arrived, I expect. Probably long before mine too. For all we know, the island itself may have been here forever. But it became 'Bermooda' when your ancestors arrived on the Hortica over three hundred years ago and set up our society. A new age…

for all creatures who dwell here. Since then, your race has greatly populated this island. For years, we've all lived in harmony with the island and with each other. A peaceful Moo-topia."

Out of the corner of his eye, Chuck saw Dakota raising his hand. KICK!—He hoofed Dakota in the leg. *Didn't I just tell him to keep quiet?* Chuck thought to himself.

Dakota spoke up anyway, "Don't you ever worry that humans will find your island?"—KICK!—"I mean, this island?"—KICK!—"I mean, *our* island?"

"Of course not," Cornelius hooted. "How ridiculous! Hu'mans haven't existed for hundreds of years. They are...extinct."

"Extinct?" Dakota echoed.

"Yes, young one," Cornelius answered, adjusting his monocle. "Extinct. Gone. No longer living. You've nothing to fear."

"But what if they're not extinct?" Chuck asked. All his classmates groaned. This was not the first time they'd heard Chuck ask that question. "What if there are more hu'mans out there? After all, they had to come from somewhere, and they had to be going somewhere. Don't you ever wonder what else is out there?"

Cornelius closed his eyes with annoyance. "There is nothing else out there," he said sharply. "In over three hundred years, not a single living soul has ever appeared on this island that didn't belong here."

He directed the calves' attention to a skeleton on display behind them.

"This is what is left of hu'mans!"

"Holy cow!" Dakota blurted out. The entire museum fell silent as everyone turned their heads and stared at Dakota with their jaws hanging wide open. "I mean, umm...*wow*," Dakota corrected himself. "Oh, wow!"

Dakota examined the bizarre skeleton. Cornelius said it was a hu'man skeleton, but some of the bones were out of place and Dakota could tell there were many bones added that weren't even human. The jaw was three times bigger than normal, and it was filled with ugly, razor-sharp teeth. Each hand had long, pointed claws at the ends of the fingers.

Hu'manus
Terriblus

Boney spikes stuck out like daggers along a hunched spine that led down to a whip-like tail. This looked less like a like a human and more like…a monster.

"This is all wrong!" Dakota whispered to Chuck as the rest of the class shuddered and moved on. "Has anyone on this island ever even seen a human?"

"I guess not," Chuck said, scratching his head. "We always assumed everything in the museum was true. But I know you don't look anything like this. I wouldn't be surprised if that *Art of Cookery* book was all wrong too. Maybe everything we know about hu'mans is wrong."

Chuck ran his hooves over the artifacts on

display. *That skeleton isn't the only thing Cornelius is wrong about,* he thought to himself. *There is another world out there, and I have living proof standing right here in front of me.* He gazed up at the Hortica sign. If only there were some way he could get this hu'man back out there, he might have a chance to find out more about that world. His tail began to twitch wildly.

"I have an idea!" he said. "The first hu'mans were on a boat. You fell off of a boat. So in order to find out where you came from, we just need..."

Dakota waited silently for the answer.

Chuck rolled his eyes in frustration. "A *boat!*"

After class had been dismissed for the day, Chuck and Dakota went to the beach and set about building a raft with whatever they could find that would float. The raft was made of sealed bamboo stalks and hollow tree trunks, and lashed together with vines. It was fitted with a small canvas sail, and even had a small canopy to stay out of the sun.

"We should name it," Chuck said as they

dragged their masterpiece through the sand to the shore. "I've heard it's bad luck to have a ship without a name."

"This isn't a ship," Dakota said. "It's barely even a boat. This is a raft. Besides, having a name didn't do much to help the Hortica."

The sky was clear, and the wind was steady. It seemed like a good day for sailing. They dropped the raft into the surf, where it bobbed slightly.

"Well...at least it floats," Dakota

announced. He took a deep breath and looked at the rough waves. "Do you really think this will work?" he asked doubtfully.

"Sure it will work! All you have to do is paddle out past these waves and keep going in that direction," Chuck said, pointing a hoof to the south. He really had no idea if he was right, but this was near where he had found Dakota, so it seemed like as good a direction as any. "Your family is probably out there looking for you right now! I'm sure they'll find you sooner or later. And when they do, you can all come back here to visit! Maybe you could even take me back to visit you!"

Dakota's brow wrinkled with concern as he climbed aboard the raft. "Don't worry!"

Chuck said, handing him a boat paddle and Dakota's orange life ring. He pushed on the raft with his hoof, shoving it off into the water. "Just keep going that way!" he shouted.

Chuck watched the raft get smaller and smaller as Dakota struggled to paddle against the waves. He had to admit that he was just a little jealous. There was a big part of him that wished he were the one sailing off on a raft. After all, the hu'man world was real, and now he knew it. How could he stay here?

Meanwhile, Dakota was having his own problems. The wind and the current were much stronger than Chuck had thought. The waves were washing over the raft, soaking Dakota's feet. Sea spray suddenly splashed up into Dakota's face so he couldn't see. He dropped the boat paddle, which immediately floated away. Dakota was now helpless as the raft was at the mercy of the sea.

"Hey!" Chuck shouted from the shore. "You're going the wrong way!" But Dakota only waved his arms frantically as the current swept him around the side of the island.

Chuck ran along the shore, chasing the raft. He looked ahead and saw that even though the waves were bringing the raft back to shore, it was headed straight for jagged rocks. Chuck started wading out into the water, trying to get to the raft. He hadn't become friends with a hu'man just so he could get smashed up!

From the raft, Dakota could see Chuck

swimming out into the waves crashing all around the rocks. *Is that cow mad?* Dakota thought. *He'll get himself killed!* Sure enough, Chuck had hardly made it to the rocks before the rough water was too much for him. His head started to sink below the water just as the raft approached.

Clutching the orange life ring, Dakota dove off of the raft moments before it crashed, splintering apart on the rocks. He plunged his hand into the water and grabbed Chuck by the shirt collar, pulling him up onto the life ring. Both of them kicked and paddled until they got close enough for a big wave to spit them up onto the shore.

Chuck and Dakota crawled out of the surf and onto the beach, soaking wet and panting for air.

"See?" Chuck said, spitting out a mouthful of seawater. "I told you it's bad luck to have a ship without a name."

After drying off, Chuck decided they needed a break while he thought up a new plan. Besides, the hu'man had saved his life. Chuck felt like he at least owed him a treat.

They took a walk to the edge of the village, right in front of Bullhorn Bay. There they stopped at a café that was set up on the beach. There were a dozen or so tables, each covered with little straw roofs. In the middle of the café was a curved bamboo counter, with a jaunty sign that read *Leatherneck's Grill.* Music played loudly over a big chatterbox as a beefy cow stood behind the counter, greeting them in a deep voice.

"Hey there, little ones. What can I get you?"

Was Dakota supposed to order something? He leaned to Chuck and whispered, "Milk?"

Chuck wrinkled his brow. "What are you, a newborn?" He turned back to the big cow behind the counter. "Lo'hai, Leatherneck. Two mango juices, please. And some grilled pineapple. Moohalo!"

Chuck and Dakota sat at a small table listening to the chatterbox while they tried to think up a new idea.

“Okay, so the raft didn’t work out,” Chuck admitted. “But don’t worry. I’ll get you back out there.” He leaned his chin on his hoof and let out a sad sigh. “You’re so lucky,” he moaned. “I wish I could get out there.”

Dakota sipped his mango juice and took in all the beautiful surroundings of Bermooda. The salty smell of the sea, the palm trees blowing gently in the warm breeze, the sound of seagulls cawing over the rolling waves…it was all very relaxing. He couldn’t understand why Chuck wanted to leave so badly.

“Most humans spend their whole lives wishing for a place like this,” Dakota told him. “It’s like paradise.”

"I know!" Chuck said. "Isn't it boring?" He thoughtfully chewed on a stalk of sea grass. "Anyway, I'm sure a boat must be looking for you somewhere. I just wish there was some way of knowing what's going on out there."

No sooner had Chuck finished his thought than a familiar voice came over the chatterbox: *Hey kids, this is Angus Atkins on WKUD, bringing you all the music...all the news...everything that's going on out there!*

Chuck's eyebrows rose. His tail twitched. "I have an idea!" he said. "If there's anything out there, it would be in the news. And if you want the news, there's no better source than Angus Atkins."

He pointed to the top of Mount Maverick. "We're going up to WKUD."

The WKUD radio station was all the way at the top of the mountain, so it could be heard by chatterboxes all over the island. It wasn't hard to get to, but it was a lengthy walk, so Chuck suggested they start right away. While they hiked up the winding road, Chuck had something important to teach Dakota.

"It's not enough for you to look like a cow," he said. Dakota still didn't think his costume looked at all like a cow, but it had managed to fool everyone so far.

"You have to be able to moo," Chuck continued. "If you can't moo, someone will eventually find out what you are. Come on, give me your best moo."

"Mooooooo..." Dakota said.

"No, no," Chuck corrected him. "You're using your mouth too much. Let the sound come from down in your throat."

Dakota didn't understand. He tried to moo with his throat. It started out as a moo, but it ended up sounding like he was coughing up a hairball. It was awful.

Chuck shook his head and just told Dakota to keep practicing. Dakota thought it was awfully nice of Chuck to be going through so much trouble to help him.

"You're hilarious," Chuck told him. "I don't usually get to have this much fun."

"Don't you have fun with your friends?" Dakota asked.

Chuck didn't answer right away. He just stopped in the middle of the road and pawed a hoof at the ground. "I don't really have many friends," he admitted. "They just don't like to dream as much as I do! I'm kind of an outcast."

"I understand," Dakota reassured him. "I'm an outcast too."

"Not for long," Chuck said, perking up. "We'll figure this out and get you back to your kine in no time."

"My kind?" Dakota asked, as they started walking again.

"Not kind," Chuck said, rolling his eyes. "Kine. It's a group of cows you come from. Your kine is your family."

Dakota didn't say much for the rest of the trip after that. He walked mostly in silence until they got to the radio station.

WKUD was in a small shack with a flat roof and a big tower sticking up behind it. Dakota was surprised to see someone he recognized climbing around on the tower.

"Isn't that the same laughing monkey who lives at your house?" Dakota asked.

"Yup. That's Lenny. Lo'hai, Lenny!" Chuck said, waving. "What are you doing up there?"

"Just fixing the tower!" the orange monkey screeched. Lenny was strangely big for a monkey. He was taller than Dakota, with long arms and legs that he used to swing around as he giggled and gleefully banged at the tower with a hammer. "You cows sure can't climb up here with those hooves! You're all... in-COW-potant! Hahahahaha!" He laughed hysterically at his own joke as Chuck and Dakota went inside to talk with Angus.

Angus Atkins was a short, plump, gray cow with a scraggly beard on his chin. His yellow shirt was just as bright as his personality, and he always wore sunglasses—even when he was indoors. He looked pretty much exactly like Dakota had pictured. He seemed to be arguing with a big angry cow who huffed and puffed in frustration.

"Who's that?" Dakota asked.

"That's Wilhelm Wellington," Chuck said. "The one Uncle Bo was talking about."

"He looks important," Dakota noted.

"He is important," Chuck agreed. "He's part of the herd. But I think he'd rather be king of Bermooda if they'd let him."

Wilhelm was awfully wide, and very well-dressed for a cow. He wore a puffy scarf tucked into a purple vest, underneath a dark red coat with a gold letter *W* on it. He glared his yellow eyes as Angus spoke.

"Sorry, Wellington," Angus said, "threaten me if you want, but it's my station. I can't just go on chatterboxes and tell the whole island to watch out for hu'mans! Hu'mans don't exist! Not unless you have some real proof."

Wilhelm spun on his hoof, clutched his cane and marched to the door, nearly trampling Chuck and Dakota as he stomped out in a huff.

"Hey, little calves!" Angus said, noticing Chuck and Dakota. "What's happening?"

"Lo'hai, Angus!" Chuck said. "We're doing

a report for school, and we're writing about… umm…the different types of boats around Bermooda," he lied. "You see pretty much everything on the island. Have you seen any new kinds of boats lately?"

"New kinds of boats?" Angus laughed. "Where would they come from?"

"Maybe something that looked like it could have been…human?" Dakota asked, as Chuck inhaled sharply.

Angus rolled his eyes and laughed again. "Man, you almost sound like that Wellington! He's been talking about hu'man stuff too. He keeps saying there could be a hu'man out there, running around the island!"

Dakota began to sweat under his

cowmaflauge again. He'd only been in Bermooda for one day. How could anyone possibly know he was here?

"But you know how it is, little dudes," Angus continued. "Nothing ever changes around here. I haven't seen anything different at all. Except for my stuff that keeps disappearing."

Chuck's ears perked up. Disappearing stuff? Was this another mystery?

"I had a recorder," Angus went on. "It's a wooden box with metal discs and a big horn on top. It disappeared about the same time as that big ape started working on the tower. Say, you haven't seen it have you?"

Chuck and Dakota shook their heads. "We should head home," Chuck said, turning to

Dakota. It had been a long day. "We don't want to be late for dinner again. Bye, Angus. Moohalo!"

They stepped out of the radio station to a breathtaking view. The sun was getting low in the sky, casting long shadows on everything. From their spot in front of the radio station, they could see almost the entire southern half of the island. Thick green jungles, long sandy beaches, and quaint little shacks, all surrounded by a deep turquoise sea.

This was Bermooda in all its glory. It was all very beautiful, but seeing it from so high up made Dakota's head feel dizzy and his legs go wobbly. He wavered back and forth while his face turned slightly green.

"Well, looks like this was another dead end,"

Chuck said. "But don't worry. Just because Angus hasn't seen your family's boat doesn't mean it's not out there somewhere."

"It's not that," Dakota moaned. "I don't like heights."

"Oh. Well, I think you might be here for a while," Chuck said. "If we're going to keep anyone from figuring out what you really are, you need to stop making such a kau'pai of yourself every time you open your mouth."

Dakota had no idea what a "kau'pai" was, but it didn't sound very good.

"If you're going to stick around, you need to learn more about Bermooda so you sound like you belong," Chuck said. "Tomorrow we're going for a ride in the Hawk."

# 7 The Hawk

School was out the next day, so Chuck and Dakota got an early start on their trip to the Hawk. Chuck insisted they each bring at least three pineapples with them. Dakota didn't see how he could get that hungry, but he did as Chuck said. They hiked uphill through the island jungle, fumbling along with their arms full of pineapples, whose spikes kept poking Dakota in a most uncomfortable way. "Ouch!" Dakota complained. "Tell me again why we—ouch!—need these things?"

"If we want to get in the Hawk, this stuff is the price of admission," Chuck said. Dakota was still not sure what the Hawk was, but Chuck assured him that it would give him a much bigger picture of the island. He needed that if he was going to try and fit in.

They hoofed along until the trees cleared, opening up to a big grassy cliff. There sat a small, dumpy shack with palmetto leaves over the windows and a long, tunnel-shaped tent attached to the back. Chuck knocked on the rickety front door, which had the name Capt. Soward "Hawkeye" Seawell scrawled above it. No one answered, but they heard a sound echo in reply: *Bang, bang, bang!*

Soward?" Chuck called out. "Hoo-ey, Soward!"

"Hey-yo!" A big voice shouted. "I'm in the hanger!" Chuck and Dakota followed the voice to the opening of the tunnel behind the shack, where Dakota saw something else that he recognized.

It had a clunky wooden frame made of barrels and boards. It had long wings, covered with stretched canvas and rigged together with vines and bamboo poles. It had a propeller in the front and a tail in the back. In the middle sat what seemed to be a small engine. It looked like…an airplane! Dakota's stomach flip-flopped at the thought of flying high above the island.

Crouched atop the airplane was a stout, plump pig wearing goggles and a red flowered shirt. He was banging a wooden stave into the frame, which had a pig's face with bird wings painted on the side, followed by *The Hawk.*

"Lo'hai, Soward!" Chuck said.

"Heeeey, young mister Porter!" Soward bellowed in a jolly voice. "And...a...strange little calf I've never seen before."

*A flying pig?* Dakota marveled to himself. *Now I've seen just about everything!*

"This is Dakota," Chuck said. "His family lives on a boat out at sea."

"Sea cows, eh?" Soward said, raising his goggles. "Well, now I've seen just about everything!" He clumsily slid off the Hawk, landing hard on his rear and dropping his hammer. With a grunt, he picked himself up and waddled out of the hanger tunnel, stopping to examine a wooden compass on the ground with a floating red balloon tied to the middle of it.

"That's a pretty balloon," Dakota noted.

"It's not meant to be pretty," Soward snorted. "It's to tell me what direction the wind is blowing."

"Dakota here doesn't know much about the island," Chuck interrupted. "We were hoping you could give him a tour in your flyer. We brought something for you, of course."

They dumped their pineapples on the ground in front of the pilot pig, whose eyes lit up with delight behind his goggles. "Soward loves pineapples," Chuck explained to Dakota. "I think he'd eat them all day, every day, if he could."

"Speak for yourself, little cow," Soward said with a wink and a grin. "I ain't the one with four stomachs to fill."

Chuck and Dakota sat in two barrel seats on either side of the Hawk's engine.

"Are you sure you can't just tell me about the island?" Dakota's voice quivered. "Do I have to fly in a plane?"

"It'll be fine!" Chuck assured him. "Soward is the best pilot around! Come to think of it, he's the only pilot around."

Soward took the flyer chugging and bumping up into the air. Chuck had been in the Hawk before, but he still bounced in his barrel with excitement. Dakota gripped his barrel in terror. He really didn't like heights, and this was the highest he'd ever been. He tried to swallow his fear and pay attention as Soward showed him all the parts of Bermooda.

Chuck had been right. The Hawk did give Dakota a bigger picture of the island. From the air, Dakota could now see cliffs, beaches, and coves that looked like ears, horns, and a

nose. In fact, the whole island looked like it was in the shape of…a cow head!

Soward showed them Cowabunga Falls, a waterfall that flowed from the west side of the mountain. He circled around Lookout Light, a stone lighthouse atop a rocky cliff. They soared over capes, caves, and lagoons. They even flew right past WKUD and gave a wave to Angus Atkins.

In the greenest part of the island, they saw a big, wide field that stretched for miles. Soward explained that it was Wellington Field, which produced most of the Bermooda grass on the island. In the middle of the field were tall poles with woven fans that spun like propellers.

"Are those windmills?" Dakota asked.

"Windspinners," Chuck corrected him. "That's where our boltage comes from. The Wellingtons own those too."

Dakota began to understand what Uncle Bo was talking about. The Wellingtons really did seem to own everything.

Soon they passed over the sandbars where

Chuck had found Dakota. "That's the Key Ring," Soward said. "Tell your kine not to float their boat too close to those shoals. You'll get beached just like that old Hortica!" He paused uneasily before pointing to the nose of land inside the sandbars. "And that's the Boneyard. That place is haunted if you ask me! I wouldn't go rooting around there if I were you. No telling what you might find." Dakota and Chuck knowingly winked at each other.

As Soward continued the tour, Dakota looked for boats out beyond the island. He saw nothing but water. Water everywhere. Water that seemed to go on forever. Maybe Cornelius was right, he thought to himself. It sure does look like there's nothing else out there.

Soward's voice faded away as Dakota's head suddenly got the same woozy feeling as it did at WKUD.

"I hope you're memorizing all this," Chuck teased. Hearing no answer, he turned and saw Dakota's face turning green under his cow mask.

"Uh-oh," Chuck mooed. "Soward? We have to cut the tour short! I think Dakota's going to be sick!"

"I guess sea cows don't handle flying very well," Soward grunted, as he brought the Hawk to a bumpy landing near the hanger. Dakota rolled out of the plane. He stumbled around for a moment before falling like a lump onto Soward's compass. The red balloon on the compass came loose and began to float away.

"My balloon!" Soward squealed.

"Sorry!" Dakota felt terrible.

"Wow," Chuck said. "You really don't like heights."

"It's not just that," Dakota sniffled. "When we were up there, I looked around and I saw miles and miles of nothing. No land, no boats…nothing. Even if our raft hadn't broken apart, I still wouldn't have made it. I'll never get out of here. We would need something that can travel a lot farther than a raft."

Chuck watched Soward's red balloon float farther and farther away until it disappeared into the clouds. "Don't worry," Chuck said with a smirk and a twitch of his tail. "I have another idea."

"We're going to build a balloon," Chuck said, as they tromped back down through the trees. "Just like Soward's balloon, but this one will be bigger. That should get you much farther than the raft!"

Dakota was losing faith in Chuck's ideas, but since he didn't have a better one, he thought it best to keep quiet. Chuck led Dakota to a long, tall building near the edge of Wellington Field.

Right away, Dakota could tell this building was something important. Every building he'd seen so far was made of wood, bamboo, or straw. But this one had walls made of stone. A familiar brass *W* hung above the heavy front doors—the same *W* he had seen on the coat of Wilhelm Wellington.

"We need a stove or something to make hot air for the balloon," Chuck said. He pulled away some loose stones from a back corner of the building covered by bushes. "I'll bet Wellington has something in this warehouse we can use."

"We can't do that!" Dakota gasped. "That's stealing!" He pictured the giant, grumpy bull with the glowering yellow eyes who insisted a hu'man was on the island. What if they got caught?

"Do you want to find your home or not?" Chuck said, slipping through the hole in the wall. "Besides, Wellington has so much stuff, he'll never even notice it's gone."

Dakota didn't like this idea at all. It was wrong and he knew it. But he also wanted to get off the island before his true identity was discovered. Even if it was a beautiful paradise, he was very nervous about being the only human on an island full of talking cows. So he followed Chuck through the hole.

The darkness inside the warehouse was thick and heavy. The musty, dusty air tickled their noses as Chuck groped around for something to make some light. Finding a candle, he lit the wick and a dim glow flickered. Chuck let out a shocked "Moo!" when he saw what was around them.

Chuck had always assumed that this warehouse was full of farming equipment, since the Wellingtons mostly owned farms and groves. Instead, the warehouse was full of a collection of hu'man artifacts that nearly rivaled the one in the Hortica Center. They were spread out all over the place. It was as though Wilhelm Wellington had his own personal museum.

"Wow! Look at all these trinkets!" Chuck marveled. "No wonder he knows so much about hu'mans!"

Chuck and Dakota browsed through tables

and tables full of clothing, books, tools, and cutlery. Everything appeared to have come from the *Hortica* shipwreck, and everything had the same *W* logo stamped on it.

"Shouldn't these all be in the museum?" Dakota asked.

"The Wellingtons usually get whatever they want," Chuck answered. "It's been that way for three hundred years. They've

probably had these trinkets ever since the *Hortica* wrecked."

Among all the artifacts, Dakota saw something that looked oddly out of place. It was an open wooden box with metal discs inside and a big brass horn on top. A big windup key came out of one side and a plug came out of the other.

"That's not something that would have been on the *Hortica*," Dakota explained. "That ship wrecked over three hundred years ago. Humans didn't have these kinds of gadgets back then. I'll bet that's the missing recorder Angus couldn't find. Why does Wilhelm have it?"

"Hey, look at this!" Chuck's voice whispered. He set down the candle and held up a familiar

orange ring. It looked just like the one Dakota had been found on, but this one had weathered black letters on it that spelled out M.V. DAKOTA.

"It has your name on it! Isn't that weird?"

Dakota agreed that it was weird, but he gave no explanation and quickly changed the subject. "Will that work for the balloon?" he said, pointing to a big oil lamp at the end of the table. Dakota still didn't like the idea of taking anything, but he was now willing to do whatever it took to get out of this warehouse.

"Yes!" Chuck said. "I think that might work!" The lamp was almost as big as them, so they each had to grab an end. They started to make their exit when something else caught their attention. There was a strange costume hanging on the wall. Chuck set down his half of the lamp and held the candle up to the costume. In the soft glow, they could see it had long claws on its fingers and fearsome spikes down its back. It had a wooden mask with big round eyes, big sharp teeth, and big plume feathers shooting from the top. The whole

thing was covered with stringy red hair and glittery green scales. It was bizarre!

"What's this?" Chuck wondered. "It looks like a dragon!"

"This looks an awful lot like the skeleton in the Hortica Center, except that there are no legs and no tail. I think it's supposed to be a hu'man!" Dakota said. "Or at least what everyone thinks a human looks like."

Chuck cocked his head to one side. "Maybe it's a costume for the Boomflower Festival."

Dakota had no idea what a Boomflower was. But before he could ask, Chuck had already turned his attention to a curved horn hanging next to the costume.

Chuck held the horn in his hooves with

a gleam in his eye. He was getting way too excited by all the interesting things they were finding. "Hey Dakota! Listen to this!" He took a deep breath, and before Dakota could stop him, he blew into one end of the horn. It made a loud, horrible braying noise:

*BRRAAAAAAAAAAPPPPPP!!!!!!*

Chuck grimaced sheepishly as the sound bounced off every wall in the warehouse, shattering the quiet darkness. As the echoes died away, they heard a gruff voice shouting from the stairs on the other side of the warehouse, "Hey! Who's down there?"

"That's Wilhelm Wellington!" Chuck gasped. "What's he doing here?"

"Duh!" Dakota snapped. "It's his warehouse!"

"Let's go!" Chuck squealed, grabbing the oil lamp. "Mooooove it!"

"Trespasser! Criminal!" the voice shouted as it came down the stairs. They fumbled through the dark toward the hole in the wall as Wilhelm's voice got closer, louder, and angrier. "I'll tan your hide! Come back here!"

They squeezed out through the hole and scurried off into the jungle with the oil lamp, leaving the angry bellowing of Wilhelm Wellington far behind them.

"I hope this plan works better than the raft did," Dakota worried, thinking about their last disaster. He peered over the edge of the cliff. Did they really need to go so high in the air to get off the island?

"It's a perfect plan!" Chuck assured him. "I saw something like it in science class. The lamp makes the heat, the heat goes up into the balloon, the balloon goes up in the air…and you float off back to Hu'manland! It could work, don't you think?"

Chuck sounded so convincing about his plan. It did seem like it could work. Chuck and Dakota spent the next day and a half sewing sheets and curtains into a giant balloon.

They sealed the balloon with tar and toted it up the cliff, tethering it to the ground next to Lookout Light. They had constructed a basket from bamboo and strapped the big oil lamp in the middle. Everything was held together with ropes and vines. It was a lot of work, but it looked very impressive.

They lit the oil lamp, and the patchy balloon rose as it filled up with hot air. Dakota climbed into the basket as Chuck gave some last-minute pointers.

"You'll have to pay close attention," Chuck warned. "If you don't watch the wind, you'll blow off course. If you don't tend to the lamp, this whole thing could catch fire." He gazed up at the balloon billowing over their heads. "I sure wish I could come too. I'd be the first cow in Hu'manland!"

"You can't come with me. You have a family here," Dakota reminded him.

They shook hand and hoof, realizing they

might be saying good-bye for the last time.

"Thanks for helping me get off the island," Dakota said. "Moohalo."

"Thanks for saving me when the raft fell apart," Chuck answered. "Good luck, hu'man."

As Chuck loosened the rope that held the balloon to the ground, he realized that for the first time since he'd found Dakota, he was genuinely sad. And it wasn't just because he wanted to go see the hu'man world. Over the last week, Dakota had become much more than a trinket or a pet. He had become a friend. Chuck didn't have many friends…and he didn't want this one to leave. He was so lost in thought that he didn't notice he'd forgotten to let go of the rope.

"Chuck!" he heard from above. "What are you doing?!"

Chuck looked down and noticed his feet were no longer touching the ground. His shadow got smaller and smaller as the balloon rose into the air, taking him with it.

Dakota knew that Chuck wanted to see the human world, but this was going too far. "Let go, Chuck! Let go!" he yelled from the basket. "You can't come with me!"

Chuck wanted to tell Dakota that he wasn't trying to come with him, but it was too late. The balloon had taken off, and Chuck's hooves were now dangling hundreds of feet over Bermooda.

"Help me!" He mooed in a panic.

Dakota stopped paying attention to the balloon and pulled on Chuck's rope, grunting and straining to help him climb up. The extra weight of Chuck dangling from the rope sent the balloon spinning out of control. By the time Chuck reached the top, the whole basket lurched in the wind, and the burning oil lamp rocked back and forth.

"I told you, you can't come with me!" Dakota screamed with a red face. "I lied! We do have cows in the human world! Lots of them! Do you know what happens to them? They get eaten!"

No sooner had these words been spoken than the lamp tipped over, catching the basket on fire. Now both of them panicked. They were

hundreds of feet over the sea, and the basket was on fire and spinning out of control. They frantically climbed the ropes out of the flaming basket and up toward the balloon. The fire climbed upward toward them, singeing Chuck's tail. The ocean got bigger and bigger as the balloon began to fall out of the sky, plummeting toward the waves below.

Chuck and Dakota jumped from the

burning balloon as it flailed downward in a spiral of flames.

*SPLASH!*

They held their breath as they landed in the water.

*FSSSSST!* The balloon fizzled as it crashed into the waves.

Once again, Chuck and Dakota found themselves flopping onto the shore like wet rats. "That's why I don't like heights," Dakota grumbled, putting his head on the ground. He was now convinced that there was no way to leave this island.

Chuck wasn't sure what hurt more: the fact that the amazing hu'man world was full of cows who got eaten, or the fact that his new friend had lied to him. "Why did you lie to me about the cows?"

"I'm sorry," Dakota said with his eyes closed. "You're my friend. I didn't want to you know what happens to cows in my world."

"Friends don't lie to each other," Chuck said.

"I know. No more lies," Dakota promised.

Chuck smiled. They watched a pillar of black smoke billow up from place where their flaming balloon had crashed into the water. "Too bad there wasn't a ship nearby." Dakota said. "We could have sent them a smoke signal." His eyes suddenly lit up. That's it! A signal! This time, he was the one who had an idea!

"What about the radio tower?" he asked.

"Couldn't we use that to send a signal? A call? To…out there?"

"We can't do that," Chuck said, wringing out his fur.

"Sure we could!" Dakota insisted. "We could sneak up there late at night, after everyone's asleep—"

"*No*. I mean we can't do that," Chuck said, cutting him off. "We can't call more hu'mans to the island. You said it yourself…hu'mans eat cows. If we're gonna get you back out there, we have to do just that: get *you* out there. We're not bringing anyone else *here*."

They got Dakota back into his cowmaflauge and started walking back to the Porter House.

"At least now you won't miss the Boomflower

Festival tonight," Chuck said, lightening the mood.

"What is the Boomflower Festival?" Dakota finally asked.

"You'll love it!" Chuck said excitedly. "On the first no-moon of summer, we stay up all night and shoot fire seeds into the sky. They make a big BOOM and light up the sky with giant, colorful flowers made of fire!"

Now Dakota understood. "Ohhh… fireworks!"

"*Fireworks?*" Chuck echoed, wrinkling his snout. "What a boring name for something so pretty."

The Boomflower festival was quite the event on Bermooda. Nearly everyone showed up for it. Bermooda Village was decorated with colorful flowers, flags, and banners. Everywhere Dakota looked, there were games, food, and music.

Angus Atkins had come down from the radio station to spin records live at the party. Soward had brought the Hawk down to

Bullhorn Beach, and was giving everyone free rides as the sky behind them lit up with the colorful flashes of booming fireworks.

It was an incredible mu'au—a huge tropical party full of cows. It was the grandest party Dakota had ever seen. He sat with Chuck and the rest of the Porters as they dined on pineapple served fresh from Leatherneck's grill.

Angus was just about to spin another record when he was interrupted by another loud boom that filled the sky—a long, low boom that didn't come from the fireworks. Lightning lit up the dark clouds growing on the horizon as the wind suddenly began to blow harder.

"Oh dear," said Mama Porter. "Looks like a storm is coming."

"Awwwww," complained Patty. "We won't get to see the Grand-Daddy Boomflower."

Chuck saw Dakota's puzzled look. "The Grand-Daddy Boomflower is the last one of the night," he explained. "It booms so big and so bright that you can hear it and see it from anywhere on the whole island!"

"All right, hooves and heifers," Angus announced. "Looks like we got a big squall rolling in. Let's pack things up."

But Angus's voice was drowned out by another voice over the chatterboxes. Angus furrowed his brow in confusion. His voice was normally the only one on the chatterboxes. Whose voice was this?

"Attention Cow Island. Attention Cow

Island. This is Alpha Tango Seven making hu'man contact. Repeat—this is Alpha Tango Seven making hu'man contact. We are southbound, approaching your coordinates. Be advised."

Every cow on the island fell silent, as they all looked at each other with wild eyes. The storm, it seemed, was not the only thing coming.

Panic stampeded through the crowd, as the entire village was suddenly filled with an avalanche of questions:

"Did you hear that?"

"Hu'mans coming here?"

"I thought hu'mans were extinct!"

"How do they know about us?"

"They called us 'Cow Island.'" Angus

pointed out. "They know who we are. They didn't find us by accident. Someone called them here."

"Who?" hooted Cornelius. "Who would do such a thing?"

*Who indeed?* Chuck thought to himself, glaring at Dakota.

"Does it really matter?" a deep voice asked from the back of the crowd. Everyone turned to see Wilhelm Wellington strolling toward the front. "What matters now is that we have someone to lead us in this difficult time. Someone who has studied hu'mans and knows how to deal with them. Someone like…me." Wilhelm sneered and motioned toward the council. "Look at your Herd. See how they cower!"

Indeed, the herd looked very cowardly and confused, as if no one knew what to do.

As Wilhelm walked through the crowd, Dakota was suddenly yanked by the collar and pulled behind Leatherneck's grill. He found himself face to face with a very angry Chuck.

"You!" Chuck accused him. "*You* called them here! I told you not to use that radio tower and you did it anyway!"

"No!" Dakota said. "It wasn't me!"

"What about that orange ring in Wilhelm's warehouse?" Chuck continued, as his nose and ears flushed red with anger. "The one with your name on it? What about that? You said no more lies! Now we will all be eaten just because you had to call your family!"

"I don't have a family!" Dakota yelled.

Chuck froze in confusion as he tried to understand what Dakota meant.

"I lied," Dakota continued with his head hung low. "I grew up in a place for children with no parents. It was not a nice place. They were not nice people. So I ran away. I snuck onto a boat. I didn't really know where I was going. I just didn't think I would end up here." Dakota plopped himself onto the cobblestones. "I didn't even know this place existed."

Chuck took a moment to digest what he'd just heard. The raft, the balloon...all this time they had been trying to get Dakota home, and he didn't even have a home to go to.

"Why did you lie to me?" he asked.

"I was scared! A talking cow was shaking a paddle in my face!" Dakota said. "Besides, it seems like everyone has a family but me. So I said I had a family and I gave you the name of the boat I was on: the Dakota."

Chuck sat down next to Dakota. "So…who are you, really?"

Just as Dakota was about to answer, a sudden shriek broke their quiet conversation. "A hu'man!!"

Chuck and Dakota rushed out to see everyone looking and pointing at the side of the mountain. Perched up on one of the rocks in the distance was a ghastly, hunched creature with stringy red hair, glittery green scales, and spikes running down its back. A flash of lightning lit up the sky as the creature made a familiar braying sound that echoed in the night:

BRRAAAAAAAAAAAPPPPPP!!!!!!

"Hey!" Dakota whispered to Chuck. "That's the costume and the horn we found in the Wellington warehouse!" All this time, Dakota was worried that Wilhelm knew he was here, and he was only talking about this ridiculous hu'man costume!

"It's calling for the other hu'mans!" the members of the herd cried out with their mouths foaming. "It's all true!"

"No it isn't!" Chuck shouted. "That's no hu'man!"

All eyes turned to Chuck. "How do you

know?" Patty demanded. "How do you even know what a hu'man looks like?"

They were interrupted by the chatterbox, which started talking again:

"Attention Cow Island. We've received the signal from our brother. We have your location. We are coming."

Wilhelm raised his hooves and continued to address the trembling crowd. "A new day is dawning, my friends! Everything we know is about to change. I tried to warn you that this was coming. Now you've seen it for yourself! The hu'mans aren't just coming, they're already here! Do you really want to go into this new age without leadership?"

Dakota pulled Chuck to the side. "This

is all fake! Somehow Wilhelm is doing this all himself so they'll make him their leader! Maybe even king!"

"Follow me!" Chuck yelled.

Chuck and Dakota knew they had to do something. But they couldn't tell anyone they had snuck into the warehouse, and they couldn't tell anyone Dakota was a hu'man. So what could they do?

"First we have to stop that voice on the chatterbox," Dakota said. "It's making everyone panic! What's the fastest way up to the radio station?"

Chuck and Dakota ran down the beach to Soward, who was hugging a pineapple and looking quite frightened as he sat in the Hawk.

The storm was getting heavier now. The rain was driving harder and the wind was so strong that they had to yell in order to hear each other.

"Soward!" Dakota said, catching his breath. "We need you to fly us up to the radio station! We might be able to…umm…to stop the humans!"

"In this?" Soward replied, dropping his pineapple. "Are you kidding? Have you forgotten there's a wee little storm going on?"

"Have you forgotten page seventeen of *The Art of Cookery*?" Chuck reminded him. Soward chewed on that thought for a moment. Page 17 was Baked Ham.

"Right," he agreed. "Climb aboard."

Soward got the Hawk into the air. He had never expected a storm like this would help him fly better, but the flyer was so light that the wind pushed them up higher to the to top of the mountain. Thick storm clouds began to cover the mountain like an angry blanket of cotton candy, and they were flying right into it.

"Where are you going to land?" Dakota asked.

"I dunno! This is a first time for both of us!" Soward called back. As they sputtered to the top, he brought the Hawk to a rough landing on a big, flat rock near the tower. When the three of them climbed out of the flyer, the wind tried to pick it up off the ground, but Soward grabbed it just in time. "Go on!" he said. "I'll stay here and hold the Hawk down!"

Chuck and Dakota rushed to the radio

station and found the door locked. Whatever was happening, it wasn't happening anywhere inside. Looking up to the tower, they saw a familiar object stuck to the very top.

"That's Angus's recorder!" Dakota said. "The one Wilhelm had in his warehouse! The humans are nothing but a recorded message! Wilhelm is broadcasting a phony message to the whole island!"

Lightning ripped across the clouds above them so brightly it seemed as though it may tear the whole sky in two. "We have to get that recorder!" Chuck looked up at the tower. He hoped he could get to the top without being blown off by the wind or being struck by lightning.

Chuck tried to climb, but the rickety wooden rungs were wet and he couldn't grip them with his hooves. He slipped off and fell in a puddle, with his legs flailing everywhere.

"I can't!" Chuck mooed. "It's too wet and windy! Lenny was right! No one with hooves can climb this!"

"Well, I'm no one with hooves!" Dakota hollered back. He might be afraid of heights, but he knew he had to help! Gripping the bottom rungs of the tower with his toes and fingers, he began to climb in the pouring rain. Rung by rung, Dakota slowly scaled the tower as it swayed back and forth like a water reed.

The wind at the top was even worse than at the bottom. As Dakota got near it, he pulled himself close to the tower with a grunt and hung on for dear life. Looking up, he could see the recorder just within his reach, plugged into the transmitter on the tower's tip. Holding onto the tower with his legs, he stretched his arm up above him.

"Hurry up and grab it!" Chuck yelled from the bottom. "Grab it before you fall!"

Chuck's voice was suddenly drowned out by a big gust of wind that rocked the tower, blowing Dakota's feet right out from under him. As he swayed in the wind, he started to lose his grip. His hands scrambled for the only thing he could grab onto—the recorder.

PLUCK! The recorder came loose as Dakota grabbed it. He dangled from the tower. He didn't hang there for long. Dakota's weight pulled on the recorder until—YOINK!—it came unplugged, and he plummeted down. Dakota's mind spun as he fell through the air, until…CRUNCH! He landed right on top of Chuck, who had tried to catch him.

They both struggled to their feet. With the recorder unplugged, every chatterbox on the island had gone silent. As far as anyone knew, the hu'mans weren't talking anymore.

Chuck and Dakota scrambled down to the Hawk.

Soward looked at the box in Dakota's hand. "What's this?"

"It's a recorder," Dakota told him. "This is where the human voices were coming from!"

Soward looked confused. Perhaps he'd eaten a bad pineapple.

"We still have to get back down to the festival before they make Wilhelm the leader of Bermooda!" Chuck reminded them.

Soward tried to start the Hawk, but the heavy rain from the storm had soaked the engine. "She won't start!" Soward squealed "I'm afraid she doesn't handle the rain very well!"

"Do we have to use the engine?" Dakota asked. "Can you just glide the flyer down?"

"You're talkin' to a flying pig!" Soward boasted after a moment of thought. "Anything is possible!"

The three daredevils boarded the flyer and shoved off, gliding down the mountain. As Soward expertly guided the flyer down in the storm, they spied the hairy, scaly "hu'man" standing on a bluff. Now that they had a closer look, they could see a face sticking out of the costume. It was a familiar orange monkey face, blowing into a horn.

BRRAAAAAAAAAAPPPPPP!!!!!!

"It's Lenny!" Chuck said. "What is he doing?"

"Of course!" Dakota shouted, snapping

his fingers. “He’s the only one who could have climbed that tower! Wilhelm must have hired him to steal the recorder, and then plant it up there with his fake message!”

“And now Wilhelm has him wearing the hu’man costume!” Chuck added.

Lenny saw the Hawk gliding closer and started to run.

“Soward! How close to Lenny can you swoop this flyer?” Dakota asked.

“What are you going to do?” Chuck yelled.

“Just reach out and get ready to grab!” Dakota told him.

Pulling on the lines, Soward aimed the flyer toward the bluff. Chuck and Dakota reached out of the Hawk, ready to grab the scheming monkey. Lenny ran to the edge of the bluff, about to leap off into the treetops below.

"He's getting away!" Dakota yelled. "Swoop, Soward! Swoop!"

Soward swooped.

Lenny leaped.

Chuck and Dakota grabbed.

Lenny noticed that even though he had leaped, he hadn't exactly landed. He looked up to find Chuck and Dakota holding him by the scruff of his costume as the Hawk continued to glide down. The costume's open bottom gave Lenny an easy getaway. He slipped right out and landed in the trees. He swung off into hiding, not wasting a moment of his newfound freedom.

The Hawk skirted to a landing on Cape Cud. The rain and wind had finally lightened up. Lenny had gotten away, but they still had the costume and the recorder. This would be more than enough to prove that the whole hu'man scare was a fake. As they readied themselves to show their findings, Dakota noticed that Chuck's tail was twitching more wildly than he had ever seen. He knew what that meant.

"You have an idea, don't you?" Dakota asked.

"I sure do," Chuck said with a grin.

Wilhelm Wellington stood at the edge of the village and addressed the crowd gathered on Bullhorn Beach. He felt very grand and majestic standing over the crowd on the muddy beach with Mount Maverick rising behind him. “My fellow bovines,” he said, “the time of hu’man invasion shall soon be upon us. I tell you, appoint me as your unquestioned leader! I will—”

Wilhelm's speech was broken off by a sound in the trees.

*Attention Cow Island!* it said.

Wilhelm raised his thick brow in confusion. This was not part of his plan. Where was this coming from?

*Attention Cow Island!* it repeated. *We are coming!*

Wilhelm looked into the trees to see a familiar, fearsome shape. A tall, menacing creature with spikes all down its back. A monster with big sharp teeth and long terrible claws!

"It can't be!" Wilhelm said. "It can't be real!" The creature's hollow eyes glowed like fire as it lurched out of the trees toward Wilhelm, repeating the same words: *We are coming! We are coming! We are coming!*

“Noooooo!” Wilhelm mooed, frantically running away. This was not his hu’man! This was a real hu’man! A terrible, fire-breathing hu’man! As he chugged across the beach, a dreadful braying sound followed him:

BRRAAAAAAAAAAAPPPPPP!!!!!!

Startled by the sound, Wilhelm stumbled and splashed face-first into the mud. His head rose from the muck to the sound of laughter from an entire beach full of cows. Wilhem wiped the mud from his eyes to see his very own costume dangling from a long pole, held by none other than than Soward Seawell. A burning torch at the end of the pole framed the mask in flames, making its eyes glow. Behind Soward, Chuck blew on the the braying horn and Dakota

clutched the recorder, which was still repeating the same hu'man message they had all heard on the chatterbox.

"Heeeey! My recorder!" Angus bellowed.

The members of the herd were all very confused. They demanded to know what was going on.

"We found this up on the bluff," Chuck said, holding up the torn costume. "This is the 'hu'man' you saw." Then, for good measure, he blew on the horn one more time.

BRRAAAAAAAAAAAPPPPPP!!!!!!

"And this is the 'hu'man' you heard on the chatterbox!" Dakota said, playing the recording for everyone to hear. "It was all a fake. None of it was real!"

A murmur ran through the crowd as everyone began to cast glances at Wilhelm Wellington, the bull who insisted that hu'mans were coming to Bermooda.

"Well! It appears someone has been playing a ridiculous prank on all of us!" Wilhelm said, trying to look dignified as he wiped the mud from his clothes. "After all…we all know there's no such thing as hu'mans!" he added with a forced laugh.

The crowd all rolled their eyes at Wilhelm. Dakota wanted to tell everyone that Wilhelm was behind the whole thing. But there was no way to do that without revealing that they had snuck into his warehouse, or even worse, reveal that he was actually a hu'man in a terrible cow costume. For now, Wilhelm would have to get away with his plans.

"It seems we all owe you calves a debt of gratitude," Wilhelm said. Even though he was smiling, his yellow eyes glared at them. He looked at Dakota suspiciously. "I recognize you from the radio station," he said. "But I don't recall ever seeing you before then. What is your name, little one? Who are your parents?"

Uh-oh. Dakota thought. This is it. This is where they find out what I really am. "Ummm. . .well. . ." Dakota stammered, searching for an answer.

"He doesn't have any," Chuck answered for him. "This is Dakota. He's a sea cow. But his parents were lost at sea. He washed up on the shore. He's been staying with us at the Porter House."

Mama and Papa Porter were shocked and saddened by this news. "You poor dear!" Mama Porter said. "Why didn't you tell us you'd lost your parents?"

Addressing the herd, Papa Porter said, "Everyone needs a family. We'd like to adopt this young one into our own kine."

The herd agreed that this was an excellent idea, and that a branding ceremony should be performed at once. Dakota winced as he thought about how painful branding would be. Wasn't there an easier way? Chuck lit a fire and stuck a bamboo pole into the ashes. He then used the cooled ashes to neatly print the letter *P* for Porter on Dakota's forehead.

"That's it?" Dakota whispered. "That's branding?"

"What did you think we would do?" Chuck asked. "Press a hot piece of metal into your skin?"

They continued the Boomflower Festival until dawn. It was the longest and most joyous Boomflower Festival any cow could remember. Eventually, Wilhelm Wellington left the party in embarrassment.

"I can't believe he'd go though all that

trouble just to be the boss of everything," Chuck said, as they watched Wilhelm sulk away. "I guess hu'mans aren't the only ones who love power."

"I think he recognized my name," Dakota worried. "Remember the orange ring we found in Wilhelm's warehouse? It didn't come from the *Hortica*. It came from the *Dakota*. Do you think he knows I'm a human?"

"I wouldn't worry about it," Chuck said. "After tonight, I don't think anyone is going to believe anything he says for a long time."

Chuck then realized that Dakota had never answered his question from earlier. "Hey, what is your real name?" he asked, as they walked down the beach.

Dakota closed his eyes tight and thought hard for a moment. "I don't remember," he said at last. "Everyone just called me 'boy' for so long, I'd forgotten my name. I suppose from now on, it's Dakota."

"Not just Dakota," Chuck said, pointing to the brand on his forehead. "Dakota Porter!"

Dakota answered Chuck with a deep and throaty "MOOOOOO."

It sounded perfect.

Dakota smiled. Standing on the shore, he no longer felt like he was lost on Bermooda. He felt like he had been found. Perhaps there was a reason why he hadn't been able to leave the island. For the first time in his life, he felt certain that he was home.

As the two new friends watched the tropical sun rise with the surf lapping at their feet, Chuck had to admit, "You know, Wilhelm was right about one thing."

"What's that?" Dakota asked.

Chuck smiled. "A new day is definitely dawning."